Plop, the Water Monster

By Annette Smith

Illustrated by Jolanda Oosthuizen and John Skibinski

Plop sat on the big leaf
and looked across the pond.

"I'm the boss here," he said.
"I'm the boss of this pond."

Tortoise sat in the long grass.
Some little frogs hid
under the brown leaves.

Tortoise and the little frogs
waited for Plop to go away.

They wanted to go
into the pond, too.

Plop stayed on the leaf.
He did not go away.

Bird walked into the water.

He was hungry.

He was looking for a big fat frog
to eat for his dinner.

Bird saw Plop.

He came up behind him.

Snap!

Plop jumped into the water
just in time . . . **plop!**

He swam under the water.
He did not want Bird
to find him.

Bird was very mad.

He snapped his beak.

Snap! Snap! Snap!

Bird started to look
under every leaf.

He was going to find Plop.

Plop jumped out of the water
and sat by Tortoise
and the little frogs.

"What can I do?" said Plop.
"Bird is trying to get me.
Please help me."

Tortoise looked at Plop.

"We have to play a trick
on Bird," she said.

"We have to make him go away
and never come back."

Tortoise said to Plop,
"Get down in the mud.
I will put mud
all over your head,
all over your back,
and all over your legs."

Then she said to the little frogs,
"Quick! You can help, too.
Get the brown leaves
and put them all over Plop.
We are going to make him
look like a big water monster!"

Soon Plop looked very big.
He had mud and brown leaves
all over him.

"Make your eyes and your mouth
look very, very big," said Tortoise.
"Good! Now you look like
a water monster!"

The little frogs hid
in the long grass.

Tortoise walked slowly.

She walked into the pond with the water monster sitting on her back.

Bird looked up.

He saw the water monster coming across the pond. He did not like it.

Bird ran out of the pond
very fast.

"I'm **never** coming back here
again!" he said.

Plop said to Tortoise,

"You have saved me again.

You are the boss of this pond . . .

not me!"